A QUIET WIFE

A Novella

SARAH A. DENZIL

Cover Design by Najla Qamber

Newsletter
Instagram
Website
Facebook
Twitter

ALSO BY THE AUTHOR

One For Sorrow (Isabel Fielding book one)

Two For Joy (Isabel Fielding book two)

Three For A Girl (Isabel Fielding book three)

The Isabel Fielding Boxed Set

Supernatural Suspense:

You Are Invited

Short suspenseful reads:

They Are Liars: A novella

Harborside Hatred (A Liars Island novella)

PART ONE
Jack's Diary

Chapter One

5TH DECEMBER 2019

I don't know her actual name, but I've invented many for her. My favourite is Ingrid because she reminds me of Ingrid Bergman. Particularly her early Hollywood movies like Casablanca, where she played a melancholic beauty. A good girl, always, but sad about it.

We've never met—Ingrid and I—but we're neighbours. In a sense, at least. We don't share a wall or anything like that. Our houses aren't even that close. But my bedroom window overlooks her garden in the valley below. You must be rich to live here, with these big houses so spaced apart. I live alone, but she lives with a man. Her husband, I assume.

She's a quiet wife, living a quiet life. Through my telescope, I can see right into their house. They chose the glass fronted kind, assuming the house nestled in a valley where no one would see them. I watched the contractors building it over the space of eighteen months. The husband stopped by several times and chatted to men in hard hats. She never visited. I would have remembered her if she had. No, Ingrid popped up one day, changing everything.

I inherited my house once my parents died. Mother fell down the stairs three years ago. It happened before breakfast. She fell into the breakfast tray I'd made for her, knocking me back off my feet. I'd been on my way to take it to her. She was already dead by the time she crashed into me; her neck broken from the fall.

I've only ever lived in one place—this house. My house, now. Perhaps someone else would find it too full of horrible memories to carry on living here, but I suppose I'm not that kind of person.

Anyway, I didn't start this diary to talk about myself; I started it for *her*. I want to track her; you see. She interests me. You could say that I'm beguiled, and that isn't a word I use often. Not since Lydia.

So, let's start with the basics, shall we?

I have estimated her height to be around five feet and six inches. This is based on the fact I suspect her husband is around six feet tall, judging by his height in comparison with the builders. She is slender. Perhaps a dress size eight or ten. Her hair is platinum blonde with a silver tinge to it. She likes to dye it regularly. Sometimes it's slightly pink.

She's younger than I am. I've estimated her age to be around twenty-five. I'm thirty-three. Her husband seems to be even older than I am, judging by the peppering of grey in his dark hair and beard. Yes, I can see his hair colour through my telescope, it's really rather good. The husband I reckon to be in his mid-forties, making him twenty years older than her, give or take. For that reason, I wonder whether she's his second wife. I've never seen children at the house. Well, at least there aren't any stepchildren for her to worry about.

She has a routine.

He wakes with the sunrise—earlier in winter—rouses her, and they have sex.

You're probably wondering how I know that. Well, they leave the curtains open. They aren't shy. My theory is that he enjoys the danger of it, the potential for eyes to see them. None of that kind of thing appeals to me. If Ingrid was mine, I'd want her all to myself. I certainly wouldn't want to share her body with any potential onlookers. Most mornings, I see him toss the duvet back before he lifts her on top of him. She has her back to me, but he stares out of the window. He can't see me from where I am. I have a telescope and he doesn't. Still, it's unnerving.

After the sex, he showers, and she does one of the following things: reads a book, reads her phone, cries or naps.

She drapes a silk dressing gown over her alabaster skin and brushes her hair before he gets out of the shower. Then she hurries down their open staircase, makes fresh coffee and places three slices of white bread in the toaster. She mashes avocado, spreads it over the toast and arranges tomato slices on top. The husband then kisses her on the cheek, eats the breakfast she makes, drains his coffee and leaves. He wears a suit. She wears her robe and red-rimmed eyes.

I rarely see them speak during this process.

Afterwards, she drinks two iced coffees with some sort of milk, or substitute—I can't quite read the label —and runs a bath.

She does some light tidying—they have a weekly cleaner, of course—and eats her lunch in the garden. Sometimes I hear music filtering up towards my house. The wind needs to be blowing in the right direction to hear it. But I suspect she plays it most days. It's rock music with heavy guitars and drums. Unfortunately, I don't know the band, otherwise I'd check for them on Spotify. It would thrill me to listen to music she loves.

Sometimes she dances. Arms outstretched. Hair flying. Whirling her body under the sun, her dress hitching up to mid-thigh. I enjoy those days the most. I remain glued to the telescope, transfixed by her move-ment. She doesn't dance like the women on television. There's no gyration, no grinding. She reminds me of a ballerina. The kind attached to a music box, spinning and spinning and spinning. I want to learn why she moves like this. Why doesn't she go out and meet friends? Why does she stay at home every day and dance in the garden until she's so dizzy she almost falls?

Later, she cooks dinner for him. And I mean, she actually cooks. Everything she makes is from scratch, sauces, fresh bread, even fresh pasta. They receive produce deliveries from the local farms. Every week, a box packed full of meat arrives. Then the veggie box. I watch her husband devour those mouth-watering meals at the end of the day. God, I wish it was me. Yesterday, diary, I ate a pot noodle and had a bourbon biscuit for dessert. And the kicker is, sometimes he doesn't even come home. Whatever he does for a living keeps him out of the house a fair bit. She rarely leaves, but he's hardly there. It's a mismatch. I can't help but think about how I'd *always* be there.

I like the fact she never leaves. She's loyal.

I like other things about her too. She's beautiful. She keeps a tidy house. But most of all, she knows her limits. She accepts them. She's submissive. She's quiet. She's perfect.

W hat a tedious Christmas. I had hoped to be alone so that I could watch Ingrid. What is Christmas Day like in Ingrid's house? Did she and her husband spend it alone? Or were they with family? I wanted to see if she cooked a turkey, where they opened their presents and what he gave her. Whatever it was, I'm sure I would have bought her a better present. But I didn't get to do any of that. My cousin and his wife descended with a cooked turkey and their offspring. They brought presents—a set of Agatha Christie novels—and even a small Christmas tree.

Surprise!

Well, diary, I had to race upstairs and tidy the telescope away, but before I did, I noticed her placing the last decorations on their tree. Red baubles. Gaudier than I expected. On my way back from my en suite bath—where I stashed the telescope—I watched him stride over to the tree and swat the baubles off the tree. How I wished I'd had my telescope! I saw only the blurry edges of this movement, but I realised what he was doing because I knew the position of the Christmas tree in the room.

I pitied her then. Red baubles can be tacky, but I believe I would have allowed her that indulgence. Then Freddy called me from downstairs. He wanted me to tell him where Susan, his not at all quiet wife, could set out the dinner.

They stayed for well into the new year. During that time, I woke to the sound of children making noises—screaming, crying, pretending to be robots or cowboys or cars. I often hid in my bedroom for as long as I could without seeming rude, silently seething. Susan insisted on making a full English breakfast each morning and forgot, every single time, that I dislike my eggs overdone.

They left on the 7th. I haven't moved from my tele-scope since then. Leftover Christmas cake, chocolates, and crisps litter my bedroom. I've never been slovenly, but so starved was I of glimpses of her I couldn't bring myself to move except to go to the bathroom and sleep.

There are nights when I stay awake, and I watch them sleep. Dear Ingrid curls up into a tight ball on the edge of the bed. He sprawls out like a toddler, arms everywhere. One night, she woke and walked downstairs in the dark. I saw little of her body. Naked, but fuzzy and blurry through my telescope. The moon cast a slither of light on the house, allowing me at least a peek at her shape. I wanted more.

Here are my observations over the last week:

The husband returned to work on the 10th. He must have taken a long break from work. She never danced when he was home. In fact, she didn't go into the garden once. Now, I'm aware it isn't because of the cold weather, because she also dances in the rain.

I noticed a shift in her body language. Her posture, usually that of a ballet dancer, had shrivelled. She stoops when she walks, her arms folded across her abdomen. She winced when picking up the dinner plates yesterday.

And then I understood. He'd hit her. I'm not sure when, and I don't know how many times, but he'd caused her physical pain that lingered even now.

And I'd *missed* it.

Now I'd never understand the context. What did she do? Why did he snap? I couldn't imagine my Ingrid ever doing something to warrant a beating. Not from what I'd seen. But now I'd forever be wondering.

I had a wobble.

A personal one. It led to dark days. I can't be more specific than that because it's embarrassing to admit this weakness, even to you, diary. Though I will say that I didn't leave the bed for a long time. And during that time, I neglected dear Ingrid. Still, it wasn't to be helped.

Now I make myself go for a walk every day. The roads around here are quiet. The weather is improving. There's no ice on the ground anymore, which is good because I do worry about taking a tumble. I must confess, I am quite enjoying these long walks. Some mornings I see a robin red breast hopping along the wall. The earlier it is, the more the air smells like dewy grass and the promise of what is to come.

Sometimes I walk past her house, just to see. Curiosity gets the better of me. She even poked her head over the gate once and I caught my first glimpse of her outside of my telescope. I couldn't quite believe it. There she was, just six or eight feet away, standing on the other side of her gate, on her way back to the house after one of her garden dances. All the air left my body. I stood and watched. Her hair fell loose, the ends caressing the top of her woollen cardigan. Beneath her outerwear, her purple dress stopped a few inches above her knees, revealing thick stockings, or tights. And on her feet, she wore Wellington boots. She nodded to me and then entered her home.

She no longer walked with her arm holding her abdomen. That pleased me. Her injury had healed. I was glad for her. I've never understood husbands who hurt their wives. Women need to be protected. Sheltered.

We didn't speak to one another, but I like to think that nod advanced our relationship a step. And when I arrived home, I raced up to my bedroom to the telescope. There I stayed all evening, watching as she prepared a sausage casserole for her husband. He kissed her on the head when he arrived, and after eating, he retreated into a room deeper into the house.

She watched the news in the kitchen. I haven't been

following it myself, but I have heard about the virus. I can't imagine being touched by it here, in this part of the world.

I believe I'm living in a parallel world. One I do not recognise. The country is slowly shutting down, locking itself up as society falls prey to the pandemic. All of this makes me want to go to my dark places again. My unmade bed calls to me. However, I refuse to allow this to happen to me again.

Over the last few weeks, I've put my excessive wealth to good use by buying cleaning products, tinned goods, toilet paper, and meat for the freezer. I have enough to last for months. During that time, I've been rather distracted and haven't been able to watch Ingrid as much as I'd like.

Below ground, in the old cellar, is a room my parents fitted long ago. It's kitted out with a toilet, sink, gas stove and two beds. They'd intended to use it as a panic room or bunker in case of an emergency. I've had some plans for it but haven't put them into action yet. However, I'm now more grateful than ever for its existence. Who knows how this pandemic is going to play out? I took some of the tinned goods into the room and stacked the shelves. I added hand sanitiser, toilet roll, and toothpaste.

Afterwards, I sat at the telescope for several hours. The husband never came home. My dear Ingrid made herself a supper of soup and fresh bread. I saw her baking it in the afternoon. Barefoot in the kitchen, hair loose, face fresh. I liked her more without make-up. Most mornings she at least applied mascara and a gloss over her lips, and now I considered the fact that he requested it of her. If she didn't bother today, it meant he wasn't coming home, which I found interesting. Why not? Everyone knows there's a lockdown coming. According to the news, many of us are working from home already. Why isn't he?

Chapter Five

23RD MARCH 2020

I was right to be paranoid. As I suspected, the government announces that the country is in lockdown and we cannot leave our homes. Many are without essentials because of bastards like me stocking up before they made the final decision. Do I feel guilty about that? No, I do not. I'm alone. I don't like to leave my house very often, anyway. I have my own difficulties to contend with. It's good that I don't need to moderate my behaviour for the pandemic. I'm not a person who bends easily. I tend to snap instead, and no one wants to see that.

The quiet wife is still alone. Her husband never came home when lockdown started, and this I am extremely curious about. Where is he?

According to the new rules, I am allowed thirty minutes of exercise per day. I took this exercise earlier on, making sure to walk past dear "Ingrid's" gate, hoping to catch another glimpse of her.

Well, diary, I am pleased to report a delightful development today. She talked to me!

I had on light corduroy trousers, a hunting jacket, and hiking boots. She wore a similar outfit to the time I saw her in February, only this time paired with ankle boots rather than Wellingtons. She smiled and waved as I approached, and then she stepped over to the gate and placed her arms on the top bar, as though waiting for me to approach.

"Hello," she said. "I've seen you before, haven't I? Do you live around here?"

"Yes," I said, pointing to my house in the distance. "I'm your neighbour, actually."

"Oh, goodness, sorry. I can't believe we haven't popped round to introduce ourselves." She held out a hand and then retracted it. "We can't do that, can we? It's been so long since I saw someone I almost forgot! I'm Audrey."

Audrey. My heart soared. I'd been so close! I'd chosen the wrong movie star. Yes. And it was so apt. She possessed the melancholic features of Ingrid Bergman, but held herself like a dancer, just like Audrey Hepburn. What a thrill it would've been if I'd picked the name Audrey for her.

"Jack," I replied, keeping my delight to myself as

much as possible. I was sure that my face had turned puce with excitement.

"It's lovely to meet you." She smiled and her blue eyes glowed like warm waves. "I hope you and your family are okay. It's terrible right now, isn't it?"

I nodded sombrely. "I live alone, so I don't have anyone to worry about." My cousin called a few days ago to check on me, but I didn't mention that. His wife had developed some symptoms and needed to be tested, but I'd forgotten to call back and ask if she was okay.

"I'm on my own too. My husband was on a business trip when lockdown started and now he's stuck there, isolating."

"Oh, how terrible! Where is he?"

"Sydney," she said.

"Do you know when he might be able to come home?"

She shook her head. "No. Haven't a clue. We'll have to play things by ear, I suppose." She rubbed her hands together as though cold. "Have you got everything? Toilet roll and so on?"

"Actually, I have a bit of a surplus. I must confess I stocked up a few weeks ago. I had a feeling something like this might happen."

"You have good instincts," she said, leaning forward. "You must be very intuitive."

"Oh, I'm not sure about that." I let out a hurried laugh, trying to hide the enormous sense of pride swelling up from my stomach.

She suddenly blinked, stared up at the sky, and winced. Then her skin turned ashen grey, and she staggered back.

"Are you all right?" I lifted a tentative hand towards her before remembering that I shouldn't touch a stranger right now.

Audrey placed her hands on her knees, pulled in three deep breaths, and then lifted her face. "So sorry about that." She moved back towards the gate. "I'm on some medication, and it causes me to hallucinate. I just saw the clouds melting. Oh, and now the wall is moving. I should probably go." She backed away from me. "I may call on you for toilet roll soon." She laughed, and trotted away, back into her garden, her steps unsteady.

Well, diary, I rushed home, practically running all the way to the house. Huffing and puffing, I galloped up the stairs, still in my boots, and immediately trained the telescope on Audrey's garden. There she was, spinning, spinning, spinning.

Audrey slept in today. I rose before dawn, as I always do, to watch her wake. But she slept in. And when she woke, a smile stretched her lips from ear to ear. She raised her arms and arched her back, feet pushing the duvet away. It was 8:30am. She ate ice cream for breakfast and watched television in her silk pyjamas. Then she put on a long cardigan and walked the perimeter of her garden with a cup of coffee in her hands.

Around lunchtime, she dressed and ate a slice of toast before heading to the hallway. I watched her remove a pair of ankle boots from her shoe cupboard. She slipped them on and left the house. I trained the telescope on her, as she walked up the road. After a few minutes, I realised something. She was heading straight towards my house.

Diary, what a panic. Like a bolt of lightning to my chest. I had on my dirty pyjamas, with my hair unwashed and uncombed. I raced through to the bathroom, where I did what I could. Then I tugged on my trousers and an ironed shirt before hurrying down to the ground floor. I had to give myself a bit of a talking to in order to calm my breathing. I regarded the rest of the house with dismay. I hadn't dusted or vacuumed for over a month. I cringed at the sight of the dirty dishes in the sink and the trail of biscuit crumbs along the surface of the kitchen counter. But she wasn't allowed inside. She'd see nothing but the red-tiled hallway behind the front door and luckily, it was tidy.

I hovered in that corridor, waiting. What if she didn't come here at all? What if she turned right at the small junction down the road? I had a inkling she wouldn't, and then I remembered what she'd said about me being *intuitive*.

The doorbell rang. I forced myself to wait twenty seconds before answering.

"Hi Jack." She took a tentative step back. "I hope I'm not interrupting you at work or anything."

"Not at all," I said, failing to inform her I have no job. I have nothing, no purpose, just a lot of money that I didn't make.

"Oh good. I'm glad. Actually, I'm here for a cheeky reason. I know what you're thinking."

She couldn't possibly guess my thoughts. She could never know the sheer ecstasy of simply being in her presence.

"I've been a terrible neighbour and never introduced myself. Now here I am asking for a favour. What a shitty person." She feigned a grimace. "But I've run out of loo paper. Could I borrow a roll or two?"

I'm not sure I could hide the smile spreading across my lips. This was my opportunity to *help* her. To be of service. "Of course. Wait here and I'll go and get some."

As I turned to leave, I allowed the door to fall closed quickly, preventing her from seeing inside. I didn't want her to see the dead Christmas tree in the living room or smell the lingering scents of old pot noodles and cold teabags I'd left by the sink. Audrey could *never* see those shameful things.

A moment or two later, I returned with a four pack of toilet roll and placed it on the doorstep for her to take. I'd considered giving her more, since I had plenty, but I figured that might arouse some suspicion. It wouldn't be normal to offer her a large amount of anything—we hardly knew each other. At least from her perspective, we don't.

"Are you sure this is okay?" she asked. "I could just take one."

I waved a hand. "It's totally fine."

She lifted the package and idly tossed it from one hand to the other. "Perhaps we should exchange phone numbers. In case of emergency."

Again, I tried to hide my delight, but I was sure my blush-prone skin betrayed me. "Great idea." I fished my mobile phone out from my pocket and waited for her to read me her number. I confess, I stumbled through mine, not just because I was nervous to be in her presence, but because I rarely had an occasion to recite my phone number.

"Fab." She pushed the oblong back into her pocket. "Don't be a stranger, okay?"

I observed a sense of pleading emanating from her eyes. They widened, and that melancholic expression I'd first fallen for drifted over her features like a soft satin curtain rippling to the ground. It hit me with a jolt—she was lonely. We were both lonely.

"I won't," I said. My throat turned dry at the thought. Excitement and fear rushing through me in equal measure. "Have you heard when your husband will be coming home? I heard on the news that the government is working to get stranded people back into the country."

She drummed the toilet roll package with her fingers. "It's the weirdest thing. I haven't heard from him. Sam isn't always great at keeping in touch, but he usually emails or calls every few days. Since he told me he couldn't get a flight home, he's been silent. Actually, I need to contact his sister and see if he's called her."

"Oh," I said, now at a loss for words, "I'm sorry. That must be difficult."

"There's bound to be a logical explanation," she said. "Like maybe he's lost the charger for his devices and the shops are closed, or there's been a power cut somewhere. Though I haven't heard of anything like that in the news and he was staying in a hotel, so it seems unlikely." She sighed. "The most likely solution is, unfortunately, the one I don't want to admit."

"What is it?" I blurted out. Then I shook my head. "Sorry, I didn't mean to pry."

"Oh, you're not. I brought it up. I guess I'm thinking aloud. It's just nice to talk to someone face to face, you know?" She smiled sadly. "The truth is, I think Sam has been having an affair for a while now. And I believe that he may have taken this opportunity to leave me and... well... disappear. A large sum of money was withdrawn from our joint account about a month ago. He took more clothes than usual. It's like he realised he'd be staying longer, even though we had no idea what was to come."

"Perhaps there's another explanation," I offered.

She shrugged. "He's always been guarded about his phone and..." She waved a hand. "Sorry, this is all rather mundane and mostly pathetic."

"No," I said. "Not at all."

"He's never been the easiest man to live with." Her eyes drifted around the doorframe, falling onto the stone step between us. "He's secretive. And controlling." She sighed. "And he does travel a lot. He works all the time. It's just so strange that he hasn't *talked* to me."

"Have you called the police?"

"Not yet. I'm going to try his sister first. She might know more than me."

"How awful. I'm so sorry."

She laughed then. It was a short, sharp exhale. "Well, to be honest, part of me is relieved. Things haven't been... great between us. As long as he's okay and I'm safe in the house, that's all that matters. I'll get over it."

"Well, I tell you what," I said. "We'll make a deal. I like to walk for thirty minutes a day. I'll make sure to swing by your house every morning, say eleven-ish? That way you're not alone."

"Jack, that is incredibly kind," she said. "Thank you so much. Well. I'd best let you get on. Thanks again, neighbour. For everything." She smiled and her eyes lit up with warmth.

I closed the door behind me, her name on my lips: *Audrey*.

D iary, I kept my word. The next morning, I
stopped at her gate promptly at 11 a.m. and
I was delighted to find her waiting for me.
She stood there in her suede ankle boots and a pair of
dark blue jeans, resting Tupperware on the wall. As I
approached, she thrust the box in my direction.

"To say thank you for the loo roll," she said. "I
made a batch yesterday, but there's just one of me, so it
seems silly to keep them for myself."

I took the Tupperware and glanced inside, tempted
to open the lid and smell the fragrant cakes within.

"I hope you like lemon. They're lemon drizzle
butterfly cakes with vanilla buttercream. Sorry about
the presentation. I guess I won't be on *Bake Off* any
time soon."

"They look absolutely delicious. Thank you so

much." I held the box between both hands, the smooth plastic grounding me. My thoughts so often want to float away into the stratosphere when she's around. "Have you heard from your husband?"

She raised one eyebrow. "No. Not a peep. I called his sister, Jenny, and he hasn't been in contact with her either." She sighed. "I had no choice. I had to report him missing, even though I'm still convinced he's just upped and left me. The police are coming this afternoon to ask some questions." She bit her lip. "Jenny confirmed some of my suspicions, though. Apparently, at Christmas when he visited her on Boxing Day, she saw him texting another woman. I wasn't there. I was ill and stayed home." She began unlocking the gate. "The problem is, neither of us know who this mystery woman is." She stepped through and onto the road. Careful not to come to close to me, maintain the correct amount of social distance.

"What an awful thing to go through," I said. We began walking, and I added, "Have you been able to check any of his accounts? Perhaps he has a profile on a dating website."

She lifted a finger. "That's a good idea. I'll try that. To be honest, I think it might be someone from his work. I mean, he spends so much time doing it. But Jenny thinks it's a woman from his gym. She saw the initials of the woman's name." Audrey shrugged.

"There's no one at his work with the same initials. Maybe you're right and he met someone on Tinder or whatever."

I shook my head. "What a thing to deal with right now. What with the pandemic and everything."

"That's why I'm baking so much." She laughed. "It's therapeutic. Anyway, enough about me. How are you?"

"Oh, I'm fine. I found out yesterday that my cousin's wife had a bad bout of it, but she's on the mend now. She's passed it on to him though."

"I'm so sorry," she said.

"They have kids. It's harder keep away from it when your kids have been in school up until recently."

She nodded solemnly. "Not like us out here." She tipped her head back. "It's like we're not even in the world. We're untouched." She sighed. "I wish the police weren't coming later. I might ask them to stay outside the house."

I thoroughly understood where she came from. I wouldn't want anyone in my home right now, though I'd be tempted to make an exception for Audrey.

"I guess they'll want to check his wardrobe and list everything he took." She shuddered. I did the same, though I don't think she noticed.

We didn't see a single car on our walk. The weather remained pleasant. Mild, and buzzing with bees. Audrey demonstrated how much she loves animals by trying to feed every sheep or cow handfuls of grass as we walked by them. It was endearing, if a little silly.

For the rest of our short walk—she didn't want the buttercream in my cakes to melt—we talked about more mundane things than her missing husband. I wanted to ask her about the medication that caused her to hallucinate, but instead we remarked on the landscape. The churning brook next to a footpath. The name of the farmer who owned most of the surrounding land. I was relieved she forgot to ask me what I do for a living.

As soon as I returned home, I made a cup of tea, took the cakes up to my room and watched as the police turned up to Audrey's home. As she'd predicted, they did enter the house, and I noticed Audrey keeping her distance while they checked her bedroom for clues. Audrey answered questions with a cardigan half flung over her shoulders. She kept one hand rested on her collarbone at all times. I pulled the curtains partially closed in case any of the officers decided to look up at my home. They didn't.

About an hour later, they traipsed out of the house, and I watched Audrey clean as I ate her cupcakes. Then she received a delivery of fruit and vegetables. Oddly enough, she handed the delivery person some money, and then she took the box into her kitchen.

She removed a plastic bag from her vegetable box.

This was surprising. I'd never seen this happen before. She stashed the bag inside a kitchen drawer before putting the other items away.

Now, I'm not a wordly man. My world is very small. However, I have seen those kinds of plastic bags associated with something unsavoury: drugs. I could, of course, be wrong. Perhaps Audrey asked for an unusual spice or some sort of seasoning. And perhaps the bag was all they had available to pack this mystery spice. Or Audrey was using her vegetable delivery box as an excuse to acquire drugs. After all, on the first day I met her, she told me she'd hallucinated the clouds melting in the sky.

I took a break from the telescope after that. I hated the thought of Audrey being someone who took recreational drugs. It didn't fit with the person I understood her to be. It seemed far too rebellious and dangerous. Still, I wanted to give her the benefit of the doubt. I even spent some time researching legitimate medication that could cause hallucinations. But when I slept, I dreamt of her giving me a Tupperware box full of white powder.

"Take it home quickly," she whispered in my dream. "You'll want to snort that before it melts. Hurry, the police are here to arrest my husband." She placed a finger to her lips.

A udrey stepped out of the house carrying a tray of croissants and two cups of coffee.

"Don't worry, I cleaned the plate and the cup." She grinned. "Morning, Jack. You're looking good today."

Her words warmed me like sunshine. "Am I?"

She rested the tray on the wall. "That jacket really brings out the green in your eyes." She was so free with compliments. I could never talk to another human being like that. My immaturity and awkwardness screamed in comparison.

"Thank you," I said, taking a coffee. It was rich and sweet with frothy milk that tickled my nose.

"Do you like it? I added caramel."

"It's lovely."

We took a moment to munch down part of our

croissants. Then I asked, "How did everything go with the police?"

"Oh, fine. They had a poke around as I thought they would, but they suspected the same thing as me— that he's run off with his fancy woman." She shrugged her shoulders. "I've reached the point where I'm actually relieved he's gone. Sounds awful, doesn't it? To be honest, I don't even care if he's all right anymore, I'm just glad he's out of my life." She shook her head, that tumble of silvery blonde hair shimmering around her face. "It'll hit me soon. Next week, the week after. Being in lockdown makes it all seem like a bubble. Like it isn't real. Fuck it. I'm no longer second guessing myself. I'm going to enjoy the solitude. And I'm going to enjoy getting to know my neighbour."

"I think that's admirable," I said. Internally I screamed for her to see me. I wanted to learn everything about her. I wanted desperately to be inside her house, inside her life.

She sipped her coffee. "So, Jack. What do you do? I don't think I asked yesterday."

"I'm a writer," I replied. It wasn't strictly a lie. I had been published in the past. Unfortunately, my debut released with a whimper, critically panned with dire sales figures. I'd never written anything since.

"Wonderful! What kind of books do you write?"

"Crime," I said.

"Spooky."

I let out a short laugh, hoping the conversation would move swiftly on. I didn't want her to find the book in question. I remembered how one female critic called it "the most misogynistic book I've had the displeasure of reading this year".

"Oh, they're pretty tame. But I like to keep my author name private."

She placed her plate and coffee down and leaned on the top bar of the gate. "How mysterious. I love it!" She glanced up at my house, just visible above the trees from where we stood. "Well, you're obviously very successful."

I failed to correct her. Diary, I should have.

"Do you mind if we skip the walk today?" she asked. "I didn't get much sleep last night, what with the police visit and everything."

"Of course," I said. "It must be a stressful time for you."

"It is. Thanks, Jack." She reached out as though to touch my arm and checked herself quickly, retracting it.

"Tomorrow?" I asked.

"I'd like that."

We said goodbye, and I walked back up to the house with a definite spring in my step. The entire journey home, I wondered—was she flirting with me? And, honestly, I'm still not sure. What I do understand, is that Audrey is different to how I imagined her. She's not the quiet wife I labelled her. And that makes me think. It makes me wonder. Do I want to continue with my plans? Is it a good idea? I have the perfect opportunity here with lockdown and her missing husband. If I don't do it now, I'll never be able to do it again.

You see, I had considered my plan to be something of a suicide mission. As you well know, diary, there isn't an awful lot going on in my life. I have my house and my telescope and enough money to live relatively comfortably. But loneliness leads to dark days.

Mother told me I'd never find the right girl. There were no girls worthy of my love or my time. But she also said I was special, and I think she may have lied to me. Special people had a place in the world. They had friends, partners, adoring fans. Audrey is one of those people. She reached out. She made me baked goods. She dances in the garden. She has warmth. She has grace. What do I have?

What do I want? What do I desire more than anything?

Her.

udrey and I fell into a delightful rhythm. She makes a pot of coffee and brings pastries to the gate. She reads out the names of various crime writers trying to guess my pen name. I enjoy watching the way her eyes twinkle when she's so sure she's found the right name. Perhaps one day I'll pretend she's right. Until then, I'm happy to stand and eat with her as she guesses.

However, this morning she stopped dead and screamed before her second guess.

I almost dropped the coffee cup. I lunged towards the gate, staring helplessly as she rasped in air through her teeth and doubled over. She vomited on the driveway and then ran back to the house. I froze. It would break the rules to enter her property, but I couldn't leave without making sure she was okay. I opened the gate and hurried after her, hovering awkwardly outside the front door.

"Audrey? Are you all right?" When she didn't answer I called her phone. But she had to be in close range because I heard the ringtone through the door. "I hate to be dramatic, but I think I might ring the doctor or something. Your GP, perhaps? Or the police. Please let me know you're okay."

She called from inside the house, "I'm fine. Just embarrassed."

"There's no need to be embarrassed, there really isn't."

The door opened, and she stood dishevelled in the hallway, her feet already bare. She ran her fingers through her locks, putting them back into place. Then she sighed. "Oh, fuck it, Jack. Come in. I don't want to be alone."

"Are... are you sure? It is breaking the rules a bit."

"Yes, yes. Come in. We'll stay a metre apart."

I followed her through the entryway. Of course, I'd seen the inside of the house many times through my telescope, but this was the first time I'd breathed the air from inside. I inhaled the lingering scent of her perfume—orange blossom—and the sweetness leftover from her most recent baking session. The kitchen smelled like honey, and I convinced myself it was her. The purity of her.

Audrey walked through to her large, open-plan kitchen and poured two cups of coffee. She passed one to me and then swung open the bifold doors that led into the garden. She flopped down on one of the patio chairs and I pulled one a safe distance away to do the same.

"If I tell you what that was all about, you'll judge me," she said. A moment later, she lit a rolled cigarette. I noticed from the burnt edges that she'd already smoked almost half of it.

"I promise you, Audrey, I won't judge you."

She blew smoke through her rosy lips and sipped her coffee. "The truth is, I took a hallucinogenic drug this morning. It's something I do when Sam is out of town. I do it to clear my head, ironically. It puts things into perspective for me."

I glanced at the cigarette. "Are you smoking it now?"

She laughed and shook her head. "No. This is just a fag I started before breakfast. It's a tea that I drink. I get it from the veg box man." She leaned back in her chair and exhaled. "I take a small dose every so often and it helps me expand my thoughts." She lifted her arms and stretched them out as though expanding her mind. "I guess I added a bit too much this morning. Problem is, it makes you puke."

I hadn't expected any of this and I wasn't sure what

to make of it. My parents had always held an aversion to drugs. All drugs. When I was eighteen years old, a doctor recommended an anti-depressant drug for me to try but Mother put a stop to it.

"What do you see when you take it?" I asked, curious to learn. I'd heard about these kinds of drugs, but I had no idea what they did.

"Well," she said. "Aya—that's what it's called—is medicine. Indigenous cultures all around the world consume it as part of a ritual. After drinking the tea, you purge. Then, after breathing through the experience, you come out the other side with greater clarity and meaning. Right now, I'm taking a bit every day to help me deal with Sam leaving me. It's helping me figure out what I want from life."

"Is it working?"

"Yes, and no," she said. "I need to take it more seriously and actually take a proper dose so I have the true experience. But I don't want to do it alone."

"What about your sister-in-law?" I suggested.

"Jenny?" she laughed and sucked her cigarette. "Not a chance. She's straightlaced all the way down. She doesn't even drink."

I hesitated. I was straightlaced all the way down, too. I didn't drink or smoke. I didn't dance. But for some terrible reason, I found myself saying, "I'll do it with you."

She turned to me. "You would? Are you...? Now you can't go into this without doing research because it's a very serious ritual. You can't go into this blind. There's a lot to wrap your head around before we begin. We both need to spend a week relaxing and abstaining from red meat, alcohol and sex."

"Okay, that shouldn't be a problem."

"Listen, Jack. Think about it carefully, okay? Text me later or let's chat about it at the gate tomorrow. Don't just say yes because you want to help me or because you're curious. This has to be for you. Okay?"

"I think it is," I said. "There's a lot... a lot of *past* stuff I can work through."

She nodded, as though understanding exactly what I meant.

But for the rest of the day, I thought about it a lot. How bad could this drug be? Because if I could take the drug, but also keep my wits about me, it'd be the perfect opportunity to put my plan into motion. Perhaps I could even *pretend* to take it, fake the high, and use that to my advantage. Though I had to admit, I was intrigued by the idea of experiencing clarity. Of finally getting to the bottom of who I am or who I want to be.

Diary. I don't know where to begin. This last week has been bizarre on so many levels. Let me gather my thoughts so that I can explain everything.

On the 11th, I met Audrey at the gate as usual. That night I'd thought long and hard about whether I wanted to take the Aya with her. I considered every option and decided I needed to grasp this chance with both hands. I told Audrey that I wanted to do it, and she handed me a mint tea. We had to abstain from caffeine for a week now.

"It'll be the 18th," she said. "In my garden. I'm going to do some research so that we get the dose right. I'll have to contact Harry, he'll help me."

"Harry?"

"The veg box guy," she said. "No caffeine or red

meat. Try meditating at least once a day." She didn't smile as she told me these things. I saw how seriously she took this task and nodded solemnly.

I watched her through the telescope that week. She stuck to the plan with perfect precision. She drank herbal tea, not coffee. She abstained from fatty foods. Every day I caught her lotus-shape sitting position in the garden, eyes closed, a look of concentration on her face. On the day before our adventure, she spent most of the day lying on the lawn gazing up at blue sky. I'd begun to think she'd taken the drug without me.

Because I witnessed her stringency firsthand, I mostly followed her instructions too, though I couldn't quite give up crisps, and I found meditation to be a bore. More importantly, and something that brought me a lot of peace, I checked over the room in the cellar. I stretched the chains and placed them into position, shackled to the wall. I made sure every key and lock worked perfectly. I arranged some books and paintings down there to make the place prettier. I plumped the cushions and washed the duvet. I removed any objects that could be used as a weapon either against me, or on her own body. I thought about how I would get her here and decided she was light enough to carry the five minutes or so it took to walk back to my house. Of course, I'd have to wait until after sundown. We were isolated, but we did get the occasional car using the road—less so since the pandemic. However, I had to decide on how to deal with the prospect of being stopped with her passed out in my arms.

She's my wife, and she had too much to drink. Where? The pubs are closed.

She's narcoleptic. It's an unusual condition but it could work. I'd have to be convincing though.

She fell and hit her head. No, that wouldn't work, the driver would insist on taking us to the hospital.

When I'd considered this a short-term plan, I hadn't been concerned about being caught. In fact, I'd expected it, and had decided it was my last hurrah on this earth, to indulge in my darkest desires before taking my own life. Now, however, with the lockdown, with Audrey isolated and her husband gone, I had an opportunity to do this and go on living. But I had to be clever.

It'd be best to take her through the fields, I decided. Meeting a car in the middle of the night was rare, but not impossible. However, in the fields, I could hide us by lying flat when I heard a car approaching. It would take a few minutes longer, and I'd have to carry her over a fence, but I could do it.

If not now, when? I thought to myself. I could make excuses forevermore and never actually go through with my plan. I'd never get those dark, nasty thoughts out of my mind, or discover if those thoughts could lead to pleasure, and ecstasy, and if I could cure my own loneliness with the perfect woman.

The day before our Aya ritual, Audrey informed me that she'd done some research and decided we should perform the ceremony at night. Apparently, the shamans at various retreats around the world took Aya after sundown and stayed awake until the sun came up. I was in two minds about this. On the one hand, it would now be easy to take her back to my house in the dark. On the other, if I did take the drug, and I wasn't certain how I could *fake* drinking the tea in front of her, I wouldn't have an opportunity to sober up before putting the plan in motion. Only time would tell.

I'm not the kind of man to go with the flow, but that was exactly what I'd have to do.

We met at 5 p. m. the next day. I wore comfortable clothing with light layers—slacks with stretch, a white t-shirt under a light grey shirt, and a cotton jumper. I folded a raincoat over my arm in case the weather turned. In my slacks pocket, I had two pills cut out of a blister pack. Rohypnol.

I had no idea how this Aya drug would react with my date-rape drug. I worried for a moment or two that it might kill her. But then I decided the risk was worth it.

Audrey waved me through the gate from her house door and gestured for me to follow her inside.

She looked stunning. The hem of her long, flowing dress touched her toes. Her hair seemed shorter, curled into loose ringlets. Her translucent skin had an almost preternatural glow to it. As she walked through to the kitchen, she seemed full of nervous energy, bouncing on the balls of her feet with each step, gesturing wildly as she spoke. If I hadn't known better, I would've assumed she'd already taken something.

"I've made the tea," she said. "It's like a shot. You down it and then you wait for it to take effect." She spun on her heel to face me, her hands reaching out to mine, but then retracting, remembering the rules. I almost laughed, considering we were about to consume a drug that was probably illegal. "Jack, are you sure you want to do this? It's okay if you don't. I get that I'm kinda crazy and I love my woo-woo hippy shit. It's not for everyone and that's fine."

"Audrey, I told you, I'm completely on board."

She grinned. "Okay great. Let's go outside."

She carried the Aya out on a tray and placed it down on the grass. There were a couple of hours to go before sunset, but she didn't seem interested in taking the drug right away. Instead, she gestured to the two blankets on the ground. I sat down on one. The corner of the pill packet dug into my thigh. I wasn't sure I'd be able to add the pill to her tea. I was hoping I'd find a way to be alone with her drink. Perhaps I could convince her to drink something later.

"What are the buckets for?" I asked. There were two of them, one next to each blanket. Dread washed over me.

"Aya makes you sick," she said. "It's part of the process. You must purge in order to have the realisation of what you want to achieve."

Audrey used a wireless speaker to play some strange music and told me to repeat some Spanish words that were apparently a prayer. We sat like that for a while, listening to the music, not really speaking. I grew restless. She'd barely said a word since I'd arrived, and I wanted to hear her voice. Instead, I was sitting crossed legged on a blanket next to a bucket I'd probably puke in later.

"What are your intentions, Jack?" she asked.

My mouth opened and closed, suddenly dry. Was she testing me? Could she read my thoughts?

"What is it you hope to achieve from tonight's ceremony?" she prompted.

Now I understood. I was supposed to come here with an intention for the process. She wasn't testing me after all. "Honestly, I don't know."

She nodded. "Perhaps you'll find it along the way."

I doubted it, but I appreciated her kindness.

"I want to learn who Audrey Sinclair is. I've been

Mrs Milano for the last five years and where has it taken me? Nowhere. I want to go back. Discover who I was before."

I loved hearing her speak. I loved her sense of discovery. I also feared it, and I realised I was beginning my plan at the right time, because any later and she would have grown in confidence, making it harder to take advantage of the circumstances.

When she leaned across the blanket to retrieve the glasses filled with Aya, her hair fell across her face. The soft glow from the kitchen illuminated the slope of her nose. Eyelashes hit the delicate skin beneath her eyes. She was otherworldly beautiful. A nymph. Of course, I took the glass when she passed it to me. I would take anything from her. She moved away and let out a long, soft exhale.

"On three?" She glanced up at me, a wicked twinkle in her eye, the corner of her lip lifting as though in a challenge.

I nodded. I was powerless. I'd submit to whatever she wanted and to hell with the consequences. I pushed the dark thoughts away. I forgot about the special room in my cellar. I lifted the glass, tipped it into my throat and swallowed down the bitter, gloopy sauce. And then we both fell back on our individual blankets and waited.

Audrey sang over the top of the music in a clear,

high voice. I closed my eyes, listening. She didn't form any actual words. Those sounds were folky, lilting, ethereal. But when I opened them and sat up, I realised she wasn't singing at all. Her lips were closed. She was completely silent.

I removed my cotton jumper and tossed it away, then I unbuttoned my collar and untucked my shirt. It surprised me to discover that my forehead wasn't covered in sweat when I brushed it with my fingertips. I'd thought for certain that I was sweating buckets.

Then came the nausea. I tipped my head over the bucket and a sudden rush of goosepimples spread across my arms and scalp. Weakness flooded my body, and I shuddered several times. But I didn't wretch. I simply felt wretched. I glanced over at Audrey, still on her blanket, her eyes and mouth firmly closed.

No, I thought. We were in this together. She couldn't disappear like this and leave me to experience the trip on my own. But when I reached out to her, she grew further away. The idea of her slipping away, sent me into a panic. I clutched my head in both hands and rolled onto my back, my legs in the air like a beetle. My parents stood over me, looming tall as mountains, sombre faces grey and flat despite the rest of the world seemingly bathed in colour. They said nothing, simply stared and judged. I had the strangest realisation that I'd never loved them. I'd tried to love them, but despite every effort, I couldn't.

Dad shrank. I tilted forward and watched him retreat into the grass, becoming small enough to step on. Another realisation hit me—he'd never viewed me as a person, only as an extension of himself.

Dad had been a writer when he was alive. A proper writer. The kind who wins awards and attends literary festivals. He wrote introductions to classic fiction, participated in BBC Two debates to discuss the merits of literary fiction. He was on the judging panel for several large awards. He abhorred crime fiction. He hated anything pigeonholed into a genre and saw those works as the epitome of fast-food fiction. *Burgers*, he'd said, *all of them are soggy, greasy burgers*. Of course, I'd written crime to annoy him. But it backfired when the book was panned.

"They only published you because you're my son."

And he was right.

But it didn't *matter*.

I squashed my father with my thumb, and with that, my mother disappeared, as though she'd been a picture on an old television screen. Drawing my legs underneath my body, a sense of calm washed over me. Yes, I was surprisingly happy with who I was, my choices and my dark desires. The rest of the world seemed far too concerned with morality. Coddled is what they are.

My final two realisations came in quick succession.

Firstly, I did not care about anyone else.

Secondly, I would have Audrey by any means necessary.

Just as I came to those conclusions, I noticed Audrey's behaviour turned strange. She leapt to her feet and ran to the back of her garden. I followed her, carefully. She seemed wild, her eyes round and bulging. Her lips moved, but I couldn't hear anything she was saying.

"Audrey, would you like a glass of water?" I asked.

She spun to face me, a look of pure disgust on her face. "No!" She yelled her answer at me as though I'd suggested maiming a baby animal. I wondered if she'd misheard me.

Then she placed both of her hands on my face, one on either side. "You are not who you say you are. What is inside you?"

On a normal night, her words would have filled me with terror. The abject fear of being discovered, of someone working out that you only *play* at being human, and that deep down you were something else entirely. But tonight, after coming to the conclusion that I liked my differences, I simply placed my hands over hers.

"Nothing," I said.

Which of course could be interpreted in two ways. It could mean, there's nothing bad inside me, or it could mean there's *nothing* inside me, that I lacked the essential characteristics that made a person human. Her blank expression made it impossible for me to know which way she interpreted my words.

"I never loved my husband," she said.

And then she didn't say anything more. It was as though she'd just now reached that conclusion.

"I'm sorry," I replied.

She nodded, face still blank. "It doesn't matter." Then she bowed her head and placed her hands on her knees. "I feel sick."

"Do you want the bucket?"

"Yes."

I walked back to the blankets, picked up the bucket she'd left out for herself and carried it over to her. But by the time I reached her, she was wiping her mouth with the back of her hand.

"Too late," she said, straightening up.

"I'll get you some water," I said.

Calmly, I returned to the house, opened a cupboard, collected a glass and poured water into it. I was about to reach for the pills in my pocket when I realised something—the Rohypnol I'd acquired had in it a dye to make it visible in clear fluids. I paused. Could I convince Audrey that the additional colour didn't exist, and that the hallucinogenic was making her see it? If it didn't work, it'd be a waste of the drug, and she'd never trust me again. She'd probably call the police, unless, perhaps, the Aya made her forget all about what was going on.

I glanced over at the coffee maker. But just as I was working out how to use the contraption, Audrey hurried in through the bifold doors.

"There's no air outside," she said. "None at all. It's better in here, don't you think." She rubbed her abdomen as though still nauseous.

"I'm making you coffee," I said. "I think it'll help."

"Absolutely not," she replied. Her words came out rushed and breathy. "I will not drink that *poison*. No more poison for me, thank you very much. I'm giving up caffeine and wine when this is over." She slumped down on her dining room chair and placed her head in her hands. "I'm so tired."

I turned towards her. Perhaps I wouldn't even need the drug. "Would you like me to put you to bed?"

She frowned. "No, that's weird. That'd be weird." Then her attention moved to something outside the house. "The stars are back." She walked out, leaving me standing there next to the coffeepot.

I confess, after that moment, I felt unwell myself, and when I rested my eyes for a moment, I found myself curled up in the foetal position still near the coffeepot. At some point, I'd fallen asleep. I got up and checked my phone. It was 4:15 a. m. and Audrey was nowhere to be seen.

My stiff legs protested as I pulled myself back to my feet. Outside, the darkness stretched indefinitely. More like a void than the night sky. My body protested against leaving. But I had to. I had to force myself to step out there.

I realise now that this was all part of the drug's clever trick, but I was sure a gale blew me back. It seemed clear as day. A bitter gale battered me. I struggled through it; physically bent backwards. All the time calling Audrey's name like I shouted it from the mountaintops. I walked up and down the garden for several minutes, calling her. Then I saw her climb over the wall from the next field.

"Jack," she said, smiling. "I understand everything now!" She grinned, patting me on the cheek. "I know exactly what I want to do."

"What's that?" I asked.

"I want to go to sleep. Sorry to be a pain. I hadn't intended to end things so early, but I'm tired. Are you okay getting home?"

I remained still, stunned, not sure what to do. I considered lunging at her and dragging her back to the house, but I'd never been an athletic man and I'd never grappled with a human being before. Instead, I continued standing there like an idiot, watching her walk away from me. When I turned to follow, I kicked something. I almost didn't even notice it, but it made a jingling sound. When I bent down, I realised it was my house keys. I must have dropped them. I picked them up, and then I slowly walked home.

Two days have passed since that moment, and I am finally recovering from that strange night. I haven't left the house at all. And while a sense of peace has washed over me, regarding my parents and my desires and everything like that, I can't stand the utter failure of the night. How am I going to take Audrey now?

Chapter Eleven

22ND APRIL

This time I won't fail.

Audrey sent me a text message yesterday asking me why I hadn't stopped at her gate as I usually did. I replied telling her I'd been quite unwell after the Aya consumption.

I'm so sorry, Jack. She'd replied. *I feel responsible. Can I get you anything? Bring you some shopping maybe?*

I thought about this for a moment. Could I lure her into the house? Perhaps if I feigned some sort of sickness she might come inside to check on me. But what if she didn't? What if she stood outside and called an ambulance? No, it was too risky. Besides, a passer-by might see her walking to my house.

Thank you for the offer but I'm getting much better. I'll walk down to the gate about 2ish? It would be good to see you.

She wasn't waiting with baked goods or speciality

coffee today. She leaned on the wall wearing jeans and a long sleeve top. Both hugged her slight body. The curve of her breasts and hips brought out the dark thoughts in my head. I pushed them down and forced myself to concentrate on the words she spoke.

"How are you feeling?" she asked.

"Better," I said. "Good, actually. Once the sickness subsided, I had some rather... strong thoughts about my life and who I am."

"Me too," she said. "Things became a lot clearer for me."

I smiled. "I'm glad."

"Yeah," she said. "But I think there's more I can delve into, you know?"

"Really?"

"Yeah. What about you?"

I nodded. "Absolutely." I didn't tell her about the dark pit that was my mind, or say a word about the deep, deep well of gloom. Instead, I thought carefully about how to play this. I had to get it right. "Would you like a change of scenery?"

"What do you mean?" she asked.

"Perhaps we could take the Aya in my garden? There are two gardens at my property. One has views over the area and some apple trees. It's really rather lovely."

"Oh," she said. And then she shook her head. "No,

that wouldn't work. Sorry to be a pain. I'm grounded at home, you know? Sorry, is that selfish of me?"

"Not at all," I said, thinking it was incredibly selfish of her. "Whatever makes you comfortable."

She smiled. "You are such a gent, Jack. Why don't we do it two days from now. I need a couple of days to relax first. Does that work for you?"

"Definitely."

"Great!" She grinned.

I hurried home to tell you all about it, diary. Another opportunity to indulge in those dark desires I've spent all my life trying to quell. Finally, Audrey has made me realise that I don't need to hate myself for the person I am. I feel no guilt at all about what I'm going to do to her. I have a second chance to have everything I want. This time I won't fail. I can't!

PART TWO

The Cellar

A cloying mildew stench hangs in the air. I think it woke me. I blink, my vision blurred. Every part of my body is heavy and damp. I'm not sure how long I've been here. Hours? More? Surely not days. But maybe.

My head is foggy. Thoughts shift and distort as soon as they come into focus. I'm in a dark room, somewhere that smells bad. But why? What happened to me? Slowly, I filter through my last memories. Laying back on the blanket, stars twinkling above, the drug working through my system, producing odd moments of clarity between the body shaking nausea. And then... then... nothing. Then... here. On top of a hard surface, completely in the dark.

There are shackles around my wrists and ankles. I lift and drop my arms, tugging on the chains. My wrists are tied to my ankles via a connecting length of chain. Panic surges through me. I try to stand, but my legs can't support my weight and I pitch forward. I can't throw out my hands out to stop the fall, instead I twist my body, desperately attempting to land sideways instead of flat on my face. My head still smacks against a metal surface. Dull, throbbing pain radiates from my skull, and I begin to cry.

Why did I trust that... that *neighbour*? God, I'm stupid. Always stupid. Always the failure.

I lean back against the wall, shuddering with fear and pain and cold, blood trickling down my forehead.

There's probably more than one drug in my system because Aya doesn't usually result in unconsciousness. How else did I end up here? Now my body needs to expunge those drugs. I'm about to experience the world's worst come down.

But more importantly, why am I here? What's going to happen to me?

People aren't locked in a dark place for no reason. Especially not in chains. God, no. This is awful. Dire. Death is inevitable. But the question is—how much pain am I going to experience before I die?

There's a scraping sound. A door opening. I tense. My fingers idly grasp the chain loops. *Someone is coming.* Could this be my opportunity to try to escape?

A light blinks on, flooding my vision. Pain sears through me and I screw my eyes shut. Footsteps scuff the stone floor. But not for long. Then they stop close to me. Pale fingers place a plastic tumbler of water next to me, then retract. The footsteps shuffle away. I slowly open my eyes. I'm alone. I down the glass of water.

The light remains on and I see the place I hit my head—a metal bedframe. I examine my chains a little better now. Not only are my chains linked from my wrists and ankles but also anchored to the wall. I'm just about able to stretch my arms and legs out straight while sitting, which means I can probably hobble around, but not far.

The throbbing in my head prevents me from doing much more than that. Before I can assess the rest of the contents in the room, I tip myself to the side, curl myself into the foetal position and drift into unconsciousness.

Chapter Twelve

AUDREY - 18TH APRIL, THE FIRST AYA SESSION

She watched Jack curl up on her kitchen floor and pass out. Good. She'd taken a risk inviting him here to spend the night with her. She understood that. Especially considering the telescope he used that he thought she hadn't noticed. Of course she'd seen him watching her. He watched her every day, but he considered her too stupid to notice.

Audrey knelt down and removed the keys from Jack's trouser pocket. Then she strode out into the garden, carried on to the dry-stone wall that met the fields beyond and climbed it. She kept going up the steep incline to Jack's house, reeds of grass hitting her bare ankles. He had a beautiful home all to himself. She knew there wouldn't be anyone there to surprise her as she investigated. While the Aya had him tripping balls, he'd even muttered about his deceased parents. She'd listened to it all, the pleas with his father about him being worthy. The chastising of his mother for not nurturing him. What a big baby.

She had wanted to ignore Jack completely, but with Sam gone, she decided to get to the bottom of what was going on. Men like Jack always had a plan. Right from the first time she noticed him watching her, she knew Jack would one day try to hurt her.

Audrey had never trusted the police. So, if she was going to find out what seedy thing Jack had in store for her, she had to access his house. Alone.

She'd added something a little extra to Jack's tea. She reckoned he'd be out for a good few hours. It gave her time. The one thing she worried about was getting Jack's keys back to him without him noticing she'd taken them.

As she approached the building, she checked the outside for evidence of a burglar alarm. If Jack's parents had installed a security system, she'd have to abandon the plan. Thankfully, she didn't see anything over the door or on the window panes to suggest any sensors she could trip. It took her a couple of goes to find the right key for the back door. She'd decided not to go to the front of the house in case someone decided to drive by at that moment.

The Aya had mostly worn through her system, but still distorted the world around her. For half a second it seemed as though she was underneath water, and the un-mowed grass beneath her feet was seaweed moving back and forth with the sea. She closed her eyes, counted to ten and opened them again. No more seaweed. She had a handle on herself again and she couldn't let go. She had to concentrate. As someone who regularly took the drug, she knew how to keep it under control. She pulled in a deep breath and opened the door.

Audrey bashed her toe against a chicken shaped door stopper inconveniently placed inside the kitchen entrance. She shook out her foot a few times and concentrated on the pain. She'd always considered pain to have a grounding effect. It'd help her come down from the drug. If she was going to figure out Jack's plan, she needed to keep a clear head.

Adrenaline coursed through her, keeping her sharp and on guard. She liked that. She slipped off her shoes so as not to leave prints and tip-toed through the messy kitchen. She couldn't turn on the lights in case Jack woke up and saw the house lit up in the distance. Which meant she had to walk with one hand outstretched, groping through the rooms in the dark.

Abandoned plastic bags crinkled beneath her toes. Her stomach lurched. He was disgusting. He didn't clean this place. All that money and he lived in squalor. Audrey grew up in a council house that her mother kept pristine despite working full time as a cleaner. It insulted her that Jack didn't even pick up after himself.

She stumbled through to the hallway and decided to risk a light now she was away from the window. The bare bulb cast a dim orange glow around the place. She was standing in a hallway next to a large staircase with a mahogany banister. The walls were half clad in a similar mahogany wood, with dirty striped wallpaper above it. There were no photographs on the wall, but there were patches of clean wallpaper where photographs used to be hung. Wow, Jack really hated his parents.

Audrey made her way up the stairs. She had an inkling that Jack's bedroom, the place she's seen him with his telescope, would be where she'd find evidence of him conspiring to hurt her. She needed to find the room with the massive telescope in it. Pretty simple.

Once inside Jack's room, she walked over to the window and closed the curtains. Luckily Jack had a lamp next to his bed, otherwise she would've had to conduct her search in the dark. The lamp let out a pale glow, muted by the dirty shade, illuminating stained bedsheets. She took in the grimy carpet, the rubbish littered across the floor. Food packets, soiled clothes, and the worst part—all the used tissues crumpled and discarded about the place. Audrey gagged. It didn't take much detective work to figure out what Jack did in this room. She witnessed the evidence of an entitled man with the thoughts of a teenage boy.

Even for a crusty teenager it would be pathetic. But for a grown man, it was disturbing. Audrey grew up with a messy stepbrother she'd hated. While her mother insisted she kept her bedroom tidy, Nathan never cleaned his room. *Boys will be boys*, her stepfather had said once. To Audrey's disgust, her own mother had nodded along.

She opened the curtains a crack and peeked through the telescope. So this was what he saw from up there in his room. Everything, pretty much. The only rooms he couldn't see were bathrooms, their snug and some guest rooms at the back of the house. When they'd first moved into the house, Audrey had asked Sam for curtains. He'd refused. She'd found his insistence on sex every morning to be a chore on a good day and perverted on a bad day. There's always been a sneaking suspicion that he *hoped* someone was watching them. Perhaps Sam had always known about Jack too.

But they'd always had a transactional relationship. She accepted the aspects of their relationship that made her uncomfortable in order to obtain the things she did like—money. What she didn't like, was his controlling nature. Unbeknownst to her, Sam hid secret cameras all around the house. She'd found them one day after she realised he knew far more about her life at home than he should. He'd already isolated her from her old friends, instilled an intense routine, discouraged her from working, as well as other, nastier stuff. She'd put up with all of that for the beautiful home, the status, the designer clothes and the holidays, the food, the events.

Despite everything he'd given her, his absence brought her joy. Because it had all become too much. The transaction was over.

Through the telescope, Audrey spotted Jack's shoes poking out from behind the kitchen counter. Good. He was still unconscious, curled up like a baby.

She spun around the centre of the room, allowing her eyes to trail over the contents. An unmade bed, a stack of books, mostly spy thrillers, another pile of books, this time erotic fiction, a few pictures of young Jack with his parents, one of him holding a book with a proud smile on his face. She moved closer to see his pen name. The sight of that cover made her smile. He'd written a panned crime novel that, even ten years ago, had been cancelled for its aggressive misogyny. *Oh, Jack, you're such a cliché.*

And then she came across something she actually wanted to read. Jack's diary.

Chapter Thirteen

25TH APRIL – THE CELLAR

I n my dream a gentle hand caresses my hair. I'm not used to gentle hands touching me. I wake, and bolt upright, clattering the chains. The light is off again. There's no water. My throat is raw. Panic floods through me and I scream for help. But there's no one to help me.

I shout again, desperation rushing through me. Adrenaline flooding my body. My voice cracks. I start to cry. It occurs to me then that I haven't even tried to escape. Am I that pathetic?

Staggering to my feet, weakened by lack of food, I try to ignore my light-headedness and tug on the chains. I'm probably not strong enough to yank them from the wall, but perhaps there's a loose brick I can work on. Or a screw. But just as I begin, echoing foot-steps inch closer to the cellar door.

A flash of light blinds me. I blink furiously, trying my best to adjust to the sudden glow. Shoes scuff closer.

"I brought you something. Come on, now, open your eyes or you won't get it."

I do as I'm told. Two hands come into view. A tall blue tumbler of water is in one, and a plastic plate with a slice of toast is in the other.

"Let me go, please," I say.

My eyes dart around the room. It's my first proper look at my place of incarceration. Last time I'd passed out before taking in my surroundings. My stomach sinks down to my toes as the realisation sets in.

"No. Please. No."

I'm in a pit of my own making. I did this to myself. The last modicum of fight leaves my body. My head droops forward and sobs rack through my body.

That bed in front of me is the bed my parents installed. The shelves lined with food and supplies are the shelves my parents built. I stocked them with food and toilet roll and hand sanitiser just a few weeks ago.

"Oh, Jack," she says. "Don't cry. Come on, drink this water. There's a good boy."

Audrey holds the tumbler to my lips, and I allow some of it to wet my mouth. It's cool. Delicious. It's not actually water but sweet cordial. She allows me to take it in my chained hands and then she places the slice of toast near my feet.

"How did you get me here?" I ask, placing the water back down on the floor. "I'm too heavy to carry."

"I put you in my car and drove you here," she says. "The worst bit was getting you down these stairs. You probably have a few bruises. Sorry about that."

I remember the Aya. I'd passed out not long after taking it. Despite having the Rohypnol in my pocket, she'd drugged me first. Then she'd brought me to my own home and dumped me in my own cellar using my own chains. It's funny if you think about it. I'd intended on imprisoning Audrey, but she'd beaten me to it.

"How did you even know about this place?" I ask.

She sits down on the bed, one dancer's leg folded over the other. "Did you really think I hadn't seen you watching me? I saw how obsessed you were with me. And I remembered how suddenly your mother died."

"That was before you moved here," I say.

"Yes, but it was gossip. Even the builders were talking about it. Everyone suspected you bumped her off."

"That's... that's... she fell down the stairs."

"Mmhmm," she says, with raised eyebrows. "I'm sure she did. Anyway, I now live alone and there's a man across the way watching me eat, sleep and whatever. He's obsessed with me and at some point he's going to *do* something, right? He's already murdered someone, allegedly, but he doesn't seem like the kind of person to throw caution to the wind and break into my house to rape and murder me. I figured you had a plan. My chances of surviving your scheme rested in uncovering it, and stopping it."

"So you drugged me."

"Yes," she says. "I drugged you while we were taking drugs. Kinda hard to notice you've been drugged when you're already off your tits."

"The Aya stuff...?"

"I take it every so often," she says. "That part's true. On it I'm connected to the world, but my own person still. Beating to my own drum." She gazes at the wall, wistfully. I hate her now. How could I ever have imagined she could be quiet and loyal. She's a monster.

Then I remember catching her climbing back over the wall into her garden that night. I'd turned around and tripped over my own house keys.

"So you came here that night and found what?"

"Your diary," she says. "Which pretty much spelled out how you were going to drug me and chain me up in your dungeon. Then I grabbed a torch from your kitchen and explored the house. I discovered this room." Her eyes roam the walls above my head, then away and over towards the food shelves. "Then I found more."

My scalp tingles with fear, and shame, and disgust. Emotions I'd known for a long time. Since childhood.

"Men like you keep things locked away. You have secret nooks. Safes. That kind of thing. I didn't have long. To be honest, I never expected to find anything more, but curiosity got the best of me. I poked around a few other rooms. Your parent's bedroom, which is a strange shrine to them, I have to say. You should probably move on, Jack. Also, your father's office."

My head throbs. What little I've eaten in the last few days lurches up, soured by bile.

"I found your father's locked drawer and I broke it. I think you already know what was inside, don't you?"

I groan. The world around me becomes black.

Chapter Fourteen

25TH APRIL – 1ST MAY – AUDREY

J ack didn't know this about her, but Audrey's stepdad was a builder. And, as most builders do, he taught her a few things. When it came to what she needed to do, she'd had to refresh her memory with YouTube tutorials. But the muscle memory had retained. So when Jack slipped into unconsciousness from the sleeping pills she'd slipped into his cordial, she got to work. She picked up the heavy sledgehammer, put on her goggles and broke through the back wall of the panic room to find the secret place.

Then she unlocked the chains, dragged Jack into the tiny space and set him up by the wall. There was already a skeleton inside. Long strands of hair dangled forth from its skull. A woman. Jack inherited his dark tendencies from somewhere, right?

Then she opened Jack's large tub freezer in the panic room and removed what she'd stashed there. It was hard work. She wiped sweat from her brow as she dragged that through the wall and placed it next to Jack. She had to work quickly. She only had a few hours before Jack woke up.

She mixed the mortar and bricked up the hole in the wall. Then she lifted her brand-new trowel and smeared the plaster over the bricks, spreading it thinly and evenly. There was no time for perfection, but this had to look good. It needed to be clean.

She left the plaster to dry, walked upstairs, removed Jack's diary and grabbed the house plans from Jack's father's office. In them she'd seen Jack's father's sketches. He'd detailed the area of the hidden room. He'd also written notes about what to do with the room and included pictures of a pretty young woman. It didn't take much detective work to figure out that the skeleton left in that awful place had once been the pretty girl stolen by Jack's father.

Audrey took all of these things to the kitchen sink and burned every single page one by one. Then she washed the ashes down the plug hole. She returned to the cellar and cleaned up every speck of dust. She also refilled the freezer with all the food Jack had bought. Food that would have been reserved for her. She'd stashed it in the kitchen fridge temporarily. And after the dust was cleaned away, she unscrewed the chains from the wall and wondered what to do with them. Could she hide them in her black bin for collection day? Would they end up being traced back to her? She decided to drive out somewhere far away and dump them soon. But she had to be careful. Her husband was missing. The police could visit at any time.

Now she had to wait for the plaster to dry. She wanted to give it a full week to make sure it dried properly. During that time, she lived at Jack's house.

She never heard him scream. She imagined it, but she never returned to the cellar while he was alive. He probably beat the walls with his fists and clawed the bricks with his fingernails. She could only imagine the thoughts rushing through his mind as he woke up to find himself bricked into the room.

While she stayed at his house, she slept outside at night, because she didn't want her DNA spreading throughout the entire house. She'd been careful so far, using gloves, keeping her hair tied back. Most of the things she'd touched had been burned or thrown away by now. But on occasion she used the telescope—something she planned to dispose of soon—to check no one turned up at her house. She also kept tabs on Jack's email inbox and made sure to put his bin out on the correct day.

After three days, she stepped down to the cellar and

sniffed. She smelled the fresh plaster. She did not, however, smell the dead bodies. The plaster was light coloured, having gone through its drying process, but she didn't think it was ready to paint.

For another four days she monitored Jack's email inbox, mobile phone, and the house phone. He didn't receive a single email, message or phone call. She would pity him if he hadn't been such a horrible human being. But perhaps she was just as bad. Part of her had enjoyed outwitting the men in her life, she supposed. And she felt a sense of disconnection from the rest of the world. Still, she had no desire to repeat this ever again. Unless she had to.

On the seventh day, Audrey painted the cellar wall. Then she cleaned up, and she wrote out a letter on Jack's computer. A suicide note. She left it there on the desktop, informing whoever found it that he was planning to drown himself in the Ouse.

Then she left, with the chains, the building tools, and the leftover paint. She waited until it was dark, and she drove and drove and drove until she found a skip on the street. She pulled over and dumped everything. Then she drove home, and she went to sleep, and she did not dream.

Chapter Fifteen

25TH APRIL – THE CELLAR

I thought I'd known darkness. I thought I'd experienced the murky depths of the human mind. All of it pales in comparison to Audrey. I can't believe she's done this to me.

I lay sprawled on the ground, my organs shutting down one by one as I waste away. Next to me, is a corpse, which is what I'll be soon. Her husband, I assume, though I can't see through the pitch black. I refuse to touch it again. I did so once and my fingers grazed closely cropped hair and a large nose. Sam had short hair and a large nose.

On my other side, is Dad's project, the one he'd told me about when I was ten years old. Mother hadn't been happy about it, obviously, but in a way, I think she was glad for the reprieve. Dad had always had interests that Mum didn't share.

Poor Lydia. He'd kept her for three years until she finally died. Mum and I sometimes had to take it in turns to bring her food. I'd even thought about setting her free once or twice, but I never did. I didn't want to incur his wrath.

I had obsessed over her though. I'd fantasised about what I'd do with her if I'd been older. Sometimes I saved her, other times, I did not. And for years I'd drawn her portrait in my sketchbook. But Dad burned the whole thing in front of me when he found it.

I've started hallucinating again. Perhaps there's still some Aya left in my body. This time Dad doesn't shrink. He sits next to me telling me what a failure I am. I couldn't even kidnap a woman. What an idiot. Instead, she kidnapped me, and then she buried me alive. And part of me thinks: good for her.

EPILOGUE

Audrey waves to Susan and Freddy as they load the last boxes into their Range Rover. She pulls her cardigan closer, blocking out the cool October chill.

"Are you guys all done?"

"Yep," Freddie says, rubbing his hands together. "Everything's packed away. We'll be putting the house on the market soon."

Audrey nods. "You weren't tempted to move in?"

Freddie shakes his head. "It's a beautiful house, but it's not exactly full of happy memories."

"Right," Audrey says. "I hear Jack was quite troubled."

"Yeah, and so was my uncle. To be honest, I hated it here. My mum forced me to stay with them some summers. She felt sorry for Jack being an only child. I used to argue with her about it all the time about it. But she still made me come." He shrugs. "I know it's just a house, but it makes my skin crawl."

"Maybe houses can absorb negative energy," Audrey says.

"Oh, I completely believe that's true," Susan chips in.

Audrey wishes Jack's cousin well before heading back down to her own house, which is also for sale. She wants to get as far away from Jack's house as possible. And while she doesn't exactly have nightmares, she often thinks about Jack, Sam, and the poor unfortunate girl rotting away in that secret room.

Yes, she'd killed her husband, and she was lucky Jack hadn't seen it through his telescope. Sam's controlling had escalated beyond what she could handle. Twice he'd beaten her so hard she could hardly walk afterwards. So rather than make a mess, she arranged it carefully, planning to fake Sam's suicide. But Sam hadn't taken the sleeping pills she'd crushed and slipped into his beer. Instead, he'd slammed his fists into her abdomen. And with that, she was done. She killed him in the snug, behind the sofa, with a marble book end.

Self-defence.

Easy, right? Just call the police and make it all go away.

Not for Audrey. Not after she'd left another body

behind in a different county. An old boyfriend. A drug dealer with a wandering eye. She'd abandoned his body in a north London squat, a knife protruding from his heart. Back then she'd failed to clean up after her messes. All it would take to bring her life crashing down, was for the police to cross reference her finger-prints with those left on the knife. She certainly did not need any law enforcement poking around in her past.

No. Better to make it seem as though he'd left her. So far they'd bought it, thanks to the mystery women he'd been sleeping with. Luckily, that woman had never got in touch with the police, or with Audrey or Sam's sister. It didn't surprise Audrey too much though. While she'd planted the seed of Sam's serious affair, deep down she knew he'd never developed a serious relationship with any of the women he slept with. After all, she'd read his messages before burying his phone in the woods.

But she couldn't stay here. As long as she was near this house, unease filled her veins. The new home-owners could find Jack and Sam in the secret room at any moment. Short of buying Jack's house, which she did not want to do, her fate would always be out of her control. So instead she's taking Sam's money, and running far, far away.

She steps out into the garden one last time. She

turns up the music, and dances. And as she spins around and around, she thinks of Jack up in his room with the telescope, watching her.

———

Thank you for reading A Quiet Wife. I hope you enjoyed this creepy short story. If you would like to read another gripping thriller, why not try My Perfect Daughter. Or you can join my mailing list to hear about new books and deals.

ABOUT THE AUTHOR

Sarah A. Denzil is a British suspense writer from Derbyshire. Her books include SILENT CHILD, which has topped Kindle charts in the UK, US, and Australia. SAVING APRIL and THE BROKEN ONES are both top thirty bestsellers in the US and UK Amazon charts.

Combined, her self-published and published books, along with audiobooks and foreign translations, have sold over one million copies worldwide.

Sarah lives in Yorkshire with her husband, enjoying the scenic countryside and rather unpredictable weather. She loves to write moody, psychological books with plenty of twists and turns.

To stay updated, join the mailing list for new release announcements and special offers.

Find me on:
Facebook

Twitter
Website
Instagram

Writing as Sarah Dalton - http://www.sarahdaltonbooks.com/